KU-253-724

SBN 361 04660 X

Copyright © 1970/1975 Darrell Waters Limited as to
the text herein and Purnell and Sons Limited as to
artwork herein

Some of the material in this book was first published
under the title The Enid Blyton Holiday Book
Published 1975 by Purnell Books, Berkshire House,
Queen Street, Maidenhead, Berkshire

Made and printed in Great Britain by Purnell and Sons Limited,
Paulton (Bristol) and London

Reprinted 1980

THE BIG

Enid Blyton

STORY ANNUAL

Purnell

£1.75

CONTENTS

Mr. Tumpy's Party

"Now," said Josie, "I'm just going out to call on a few people. You play with Bun, Click, and have a nice time."

Josie went out. She and Click and Bun lived in a little house together. She was a doll, Click was a clockwork mouse and Bun was a toy rabbit.

Bun tidied up the little house. Click made the beds. Then he looked round to see what else he could do. Ah, he could tear the date off the calendar. Each day he or Bun tore one page off, so that the next day showed. Click tore yesterday's date off the calendar. Then he found some cards to play with, and waited till Bun came in.

Bun came in and sat down. He looked up at the calendar, and then he frowned.

"Click—can you remember what date Mr. Tumpy was giving his party?" he asked.

"Of course I can," said Click. "He's giving it on January the 18th. I couldn't possibly forget."

"That's what *I* thought," said Bun. "Josie must have forgotten all about it—because look what the calendar says, Click—it says Tuesday January the 18th! The day of the party!"

"Oh *dear*! Josie's forgotten!" said Click, looking very upset. "And it's to be a wonderful party. Tumpy's giving it in his caravan—and, you know, it's got feet, and might walk off at any moment. It would be such fun if it did."

Well, well, well—you should have seen Bun and Click getting busy after that. "We must get ready quickly," they said. "There are our best clothes to get out and mend and iron. And we must clean our party shoes. And, oh dear, what about Josie's sash? It's all dirty."

Bun got out his things and Click got out his. Bun put the iron on to heat, and Click got out the work-basket to mend a tear in his best scarf. He wasn't very used to needles and scissors and soon he had snipped a very big hole in his scarf, and pricked his paws badly.

Then Bun burnt himself with the iron. "It's much too hot!" he wailed. "Look what I've done. Oh dear, feel how hot the iron is, Click!"

And silly little Click picked it up to feel it. It *was* much too hot, of course, and he dropped it at once. It fell on his tail, and he gave such a yell that Bun nearly jumped out of his skin.

"Oh—you've dropped the iron on to Josie's sash as well as on to your tail," cried Bun. "You've scorched it!"

"I want Josie to come and see to things," wailed Click. "I've burnt my tail almost in half. I want Josie. We'll never, never be ready to go to the party. Suppose she stays out to lunch?"

Well, that's just what Josie did—and when at last she got back home, just about three o'clock, what a noise of squeaking and wailing met her ears.

"It's too late to go to the party! I've burnt my tail and your sash is scorched. And I've cut a hole in my best scarf!"

"And I've burned my paws and I can't find one of my best shoes! We can't go to the party. Oh, Josie, why did you forget?"

"What *is* all this about?" said Josie in surprise. "Oh, poor Bun—let me wrap up your paw. And I'll soon put your tail right for you, Click. Never mind about the scarf. I can mend that."

"But we've missed the PARTY!" squealed Click and burst into tears. He pointed with his tiny paw at the calendar. "Look—it's Tuesday, the day of Mr. Tumpy's party. You forgot, Josie—and we've missed it."

Josie looked in surprise at the calendar. "But, you sillies, it isn't Tuesday, it's only Monday," she said. "I've been out to buy some new

9

clothes for you both to wear—just see how nice they are. The party is *tomorrow*!"

"It isn't, it isn't. The calendar says today," wept Bun. "And calendars are always right."

"Not when people are silly enough to pull off *two* days instead of one!" said Josie, looking into the waste-paper basket and picking out two little calendar pages. "See, Click—you pulled off Sunday *and* Monday, and made today Tuesday on the calendar! You should only have pulled off Sunday. What a baby you are!"

My goodness me, how Bun and Click cheered up after that! They hadn't missed the party. They could go after all. Josie hadn't forgotten. Click had just been very silly!

So they're going tomorrow, dressed up in fine new clothes. Mr. Tumpy will be pleased to see them; so will his friend Mr. Spells, and Bits, his dog.

And nobody needs to be afraid in case his caravan walks off in the middle of the party, because for once in a way he's got it chained up. What a good idea!

The Eighteen Naughty Imps

ONCE there was an old brownie who lived inside a chestnut-tree. You would never have known that there was a little house inside the enormous old tree, because the brownie's door fitted so neatly into the trunk of the tree that nobody could ever see where it was.

In fact, when the brownie came home from his shopping he sometimes didn't even know himself where the door was, and he had to try all round the tree before he found the keyhole.

The old brownie was very fond of honey. He liked bread and butter and honey better than anything else in the world to eat. The baker always left him bread, and the milkman left him butter. But the honey he had to go to the Bee-woman to buy. He usually bought twelve pots at a time, because the honey was cheaper that way.

Now just opposite the chestnut-tree a little family of imps came to live. There was Mother-Imp, and there were eighteen boy and girl imps. And they were all very, very naughty.

They called rude names after the old brownie.

"Hallo, Stump-Around!" they shouted. "Hallo, Long-Nose!"

The old brownie had big feet and a long nose, and he couldn't help having either. He was very angry when the imp-children were so rude to him. He went to complain to Mother-Imp.

But she wouldn't listen to him at all. "Oh no, no!" she said, in quite a shocked voice. "My children are never rude, Mr. Brownie. Never! You are quite mistaken."

"My dear Madam, all your children need a good spanking," said the old brownie. "And I must beg you to give it to them at once or I shall punish them myself."

"Mr. Brownie, I will spank them when I know they have really been bad and not before," said Mother-Imp, and she banged her door in the brownie's face.

"She's just as rude as her children!" said the brownie.

The imps did all kinds of things to the brownie. They climbed a tree and pelted him with acorns as he passed by. They even took a watering-can up into the tree and watered him, and you should have heard how they giggled when he went home to get his umbrella and mackintosh!

Another time they hid in a bush and mewed like a lost kitten. The

kind-hearted brownie went to see where the kitten was—and as the bush was very prickly, he tore his nice new coat to rags! Then the imps jumped out, laughing, mewed loudly all round him, and fled away to their mother.

"You haven't been teasing that old brownie, I hope," she said.

"Of course not!" said the imps untruthfully, looking as good as gold. "Mother, may we have honey for tea?"

"No," said Mother-Imp. "I went to buy some for you this morning from the Bee-woman, but she says that she sold it all to the old brownie yesterday. He loves honey, and he bought all she had. She will have some more next week."

"That brownie is a greedy old thing!" said the imps to one another. They ran out into the wood. They put their naughty heads together and whispered to one another.

"Let's wait till he goes out and then creep into his chestnut-tree house and take the honey."

"But how shall we get in?" asked one. "The door is so difficult to find."

"We'll all hide under a nearby bush and watch carefully where the door is," said another. "After all, there are eighteen of us! Surely between us we can find out where the door is after we have seen it open and close!"

So they all hid and watched carefully. After about half an hour the old brownie came out, with his hat on and a basket in his hand. The imps watched carefully to see exactly where the door fitted into the trunk. The brownie locked the door, picked up his basket, and went off through the trees.

"We'd better hurry because it's getting dark," said the imps. "We shall easily find the door!"

Well, it wasn't quite so easy as they thought, but luckily for them, one of them suddenly found the keyhole, and after that they could easily work out where the door was.

"What about a key?" said one, in dismay. "The old brownie locked the door."

"We'll ask the sycamore-tree to lend us some," said another imp. "She has heaps of sycamore-keys round about her foot."

So they went to the sycamore-tree, and picked up dozens and dozens of the sycamore-fruits that lay around, shaped like clock-keys. Then back they ran to the chestnut-tree. They fitted in the keys one after another—and the last key of all opened the door!

Into the little house climbed all the imps. The wind took the door and shut it, bang! The imps looked around for the honey.

"There it is—on that shelf!" cried one imp. The naughty little creatures all ran to the shelf and took down pots of honey. They took off the lids and dipped in their fingers.

"Oooo-ooo-oooh! Isn't it lovely!" cried the imps, as they sucked their fingers. What a mess they got themselves into! They soon had honey down their tunics, honey all over their faces, and honey on their shoes!

"I say! We'd better not stay here too long," said an imp suddenly. "We don't know when the old brownie is coming back. Let's hurry home. We can take the rest of the honey with us."

So they rushed to find the door—but alas for those imps, the door was just as difficult to find on the inside as it was on the outside! They just simply *couldn't* seem to find it! They got frightened and worried.

"Quick! Quick! We *must* find it!" they shouted to one another. "Oh, is that the brownie's footsteps outside? No—it's the wind in the trees. Hark—there he is, surely! No—it's the blackbird calling."

As they were trying their very, very hardest to find the door, the old brownie came back home. It was dark by now, and he had had to borrow a lantern. He looked for his keyhole, and found it at once

because it still had the sycamore-key in it! Then the old brownie frowned, for he knew perfectly well what *that* meant!

"Robbers!" he growled to himself. "Robbers have been into my house! If only I could catch them!"

He opened his door and went inside his house. The imps had heard him coming and had hidden themselves all over the place. One had gone into the coal-scuttle. Another was behind the clock. Some were under the bed, and one had even got into the waste-paper basket.

The old brownie shut his door and looked round his house. He saw the honey-pots everywhere. And then he saw something else!

He saw feet sticking out from under the bed. He saw a hand showing from behind the clock. And he guessed that the robbers were still there!

It wasn't long before the angry old brownie had pulled out all eighteen imps, and stood them in front of him in a frightened row.

16

"OHO!" said the brownie, in his biggest, deepest voice. "OHO! So THIS is what you have been doing! STEALING! Well, I wonder what your mother will say to *that*?"

"We shall go and wash so that Mother won't know," said one of the imps, trying to be cheeky.

"I shall make sure that she does know," said the brownie sternly. "I've a good mind to spank you myself—but I am not going to get my hands all sticky with honey! I am going to throw you up into my chestnut-tree—and there you will stay till the morning and your mother finds you!"

"We shall climb down!" said the imps sulkily.

"Oh no, you won't!" said the old brownie, with a sudden grin. "Now come along—we'll see what happens to you!"

He gathered up all the eighteen little imps in his big brown hands and put them into his deep pockets. He opened the door of his tree and went out into the dark. He called up to the tree:

"Chestnut-tree! Hold tight to these bad imps till the morning! Don't let them go!"

The wind ran through the bare branches of the chestnut-tree and the branches slowly called back to the brownie:

"We won't—let—go! We won't—let—go!"

The old brownie took the imps out of his pocket one by one. He threw them straight up into the tree—and there they stuck! Yes—the big fat chestnut buds held on to them tightly, and the imps couldn't get down at all, although they struggled hard.

"These chestnut buds are covered with glue to keep out the frost!" chuckled the old brownie. "You won't get away. Aha! Wait till the morning comes. Then we'll see what happens."

Early in the morning the old brownie went to call on Mother-Imp. She was surprised to see him, and she looked very worried because none of her eighteen imp-children had come home the night before.

"Madam," said the old brownie, "I've no doubt you want to know where your bad children are. They broke into my tree-house last night and stole my honey."

"I don't believe it!" said Mother Imp angrily. "They are good children, not bad. If they did a thing like that, I would spank them well."

"Good!" said the brownie. "Very good! Now you just come and see where they are!"

He took Mother-Imp to his chestnut-tree—and there, stuck fast on the buds, were eighteen small, cold, sticky imps, crying bitterly.

"We're sorry we stole your honey!" they sobbed. "Please let us go! These chestnut buds are holding us so fast."

Their mother stared at them in horror. What! Her precious children had really stolen honey after all? Yes—they were covered with it, as sticky as could be! She reached up into the tree and pulled those imps down one by one.

And then—dear me! Spank, spank, spank! You could hear the spanks and the howls all through the wood. The blackbird came to see. The hedgehog came to look. The rabbits popped out of their holes and stared.

"A good thing!" they said to one another. "A very—good—thing!"

"I quite agree with you!" said the old brownie, and he went inside his tree and shut his door with a bang.

And if you want to find out how it was that the chestnut buds held those imps so tightly all night long, just go and feel the buds, will you? They will hold on to your fingers as tightly as they held on to the imps! They really *are* covered with glue, you see!

Gold for Everyone

ONCE upon a time, in the month of June, a small elf danced through the woods on her way to the fields. She sang as she went, a queer, happy little song, in a voice like the twitter of swallows:

"Gold! Gold!
That shines like the sun,
Gold for me
And for everyone!"

Now just as she came to the edge of the wood near the stile that led into the fields she heard a noise. She stopped and listened.

"Urrrrrr! Urrrrr-urrrr!"

"It's somebody snoring!" said the elf, and tiptoed round the bush to see who it was. And there, lying hunched up against a silver birch tree, was an old, wrinkled man. Clutched in one hand was a small bag that, even in his sleep, he held tightly.

"Why, I do believe it's old Gold-Fingers, the wizard!" said the elf in surprise, half-frightened at the sight of the famous old man.

"Urrrrr, urrrr-urrr!" snored the wizard. He was so very sound asleep that the elf thought she could quite safely look at him very closely. So this was the richest man in all the kingdom! This was Gold-Fingers, who was so clever and so cunning that it was said he could get gold out of a stone. He had a castle whose cellars were stacked with sacks of gold and with chests of gleaming jewels.

The elf knelt down before him and looked at him earnestly. What an ugly fellow! What a lot of wrinkles he had! What an unkind mouth, with lips so thin that they could hardly be seen.

"He may be rich and clever, but he's not at all nice," said the elf to herself. "And how unhappy he looks when he is asleep. I wonder why. He is so rich that surely he can buy all the happiness in the world!"

The old wizard had hardly any hair on his head. He had so many lines and wrinkles on his face that it was quite impossible to count them. The elf tried to, but she gave it up when she got to forty-nine.

She got tired of looking at such an ugly, miserable fellow. She stood up and began to dance lightly again, forgetting all about the wizard. She sang her little song:

"Gold! Gold!
    That shines like the sun,
  Gold for me
    And for everyone!"

The word "gold" awoke the wizard at once. He opened his eyes under their enormous shaggy eyebrows, clutched his bag closely to him, and stared at the dancing elf.

She was so very pretty and light. Her voice was gay and happy, and her wings lifted her a little now and again. But the wizard didn't see her prettiness. He only heard her song about gold. He sat upright.

"Hey!" he said. "Where's this gold you are singing about?"

The elf stopped dancing and looked at him. "Haven't you got enough gold without bothering about mine?" she said.

"You tell me where it is," said the wizard.

"Well, you tell me something first," said the elf, and she went close to the wizard. "How did you get all these ugly wrinkles?"

"I've had a hard life," said Gold-Fingers. "It's not easy to get rich, you know. You have to work and work and work."

"Oh," said the elf. She touched his bald head, with its few hairs sticking up here and there. "Where has your hair gone to?" she said. "Hardly anyone in Fairyland has a bald head. It looks shocking."

The wizard frowned. "Worry takes hair away!" he said. "I've

had a lot of worry in my life. Getting rich is a worrying thing, you know."

"Is it?" said the elf, who never had more than six pence in her pocket and hadn't any idea at all how to get rich. "Now tell me, wizard—why is your mouth so hard and unkind, and why are your lips so thin? I can hardly see them!"

"You have to learn to be hard if you are going to be as rich as I am," said the wizard. "Soft people are foolish! The clever ones are never too kind or generous. A little hardness stiffens people up. If they don't pay me their rent, out they go! If they don't pay me their bills, into prison they're thrown! That soon teaches them to be sensible."

"I suppose you must have done many hard, unkind things to make your face like that," said the elf. "What do you use your gold for, wizard? To buy happiness?"

The wizard frowned, and his shaggy brows came right over his piercing eyes. "I have tried to buy happiness," he said. "I've tried to buy love, too, and friends."

"Well, you don't *look* happy!" said the elf.

"It's queer," said the wizard, "but it seems that the things I'd like, now that I'm old, aren't to be bought with gold. I can't seem to buy even a small bit of love with it."

"I've got plenty of love," said the elf. "My mother loves me and my brothers and sisters. My old aunt loves me and so do all my friends. But I don't pay them gold for it, of course. I haven't any."

"Well, why did you sing that song about gold for you and everyone?" asked the wizard impatiently. "Didn't you mean it?"

"Of course I meant it," said the elf, and she stood up and began to dance again. "It's marvellous gold—gold that shines and glows, gold that stretches for miles, gold that I shall store away for ever and ever."

The wizard's eyes gleamed. He got up and took hold of the elf roughly. "Now you just show me where this gold is!" he cried. "If it belongs to everyone, it's mine, too. I shall store it away, like you."

The elf cried out, but the wizard would not take his cruel fingers from her small arm. "Well, come with me," she said. "I'll show you. It's the most beautiful gold in the world."

She climbed over the stile, ran across a lane, and then made her way through a gap in a hawthorn hedge there. Beyond lay a great field of buttercups, all blossoming in a glory of yellow gold.

"There you are!" said the elf, waving her tiny hand at the gleaming flowers. "There's my gold—and yours if you want it—and everyone's. Did you ever see such a wonderful sight in your life? But oh, wizard, don't take it away; leave it here for everyone to see and love!"

The wizard stared at the buttercups, that stretched away in a great golden carpet. His face grew hard.

"So this is your gold!" he cried, and he kicked at the buttercups. "What a stupid joke! You naughty little storyteller—you said you had gold that you were going to store away for ever!"

"And so I am!" cried the elf, stamping her foot on the grass. "I shall store it away in my memory, tuck the picture of this buttercup

field into my mind, and remember it for ever and ever! Look at it, look at it, Gold-Fingers—surely you love it, too, and want to store it away?"

"Bah!" said the wizard and trampled down the nearest buttercups.

"You're mad! What are buttercups? Just weeds. And you make all this song and dance about them. You don't know what gold is. I do!"

And without another glance at the gleaming, golden field the wizard turned away, muttering and grumbling, hugging his small bag of gold to himself. The elf flung herself down on the grass and, with tears in her eyes, began to straighten the bruised stalks of the buttercups. The wizard heard her sobbing and turned round.

"Little stupid!" he said. "Crying over buttercups!"

"I'm crying for *you*!" said the elf. "I'm crying because you're such a foolish, unhappy man you can't even see beauty when it's under your eyes! You're the richest man in the kingdom and you haven't a mite of happiness; you own sacks of gold and not a bit of love. I'm crying for *you*!"

The wizard couldn't understand that. He walked away, his great eyebrows pulled down over his eyes. The elf soon forgot him, and stood up. She began her little dance again, singing in her high voice:

> "Gold! Gold!
> That shines like the sun,
> Gold for me
> And for everyone!"

It's beautiful gold, isn't it? The fields are carpeted with it in the summer. Let's go and see it, and store it away in our minds for ever and ever!

The Sneezing Dog

THERE was once a dog called Collie, and, as you can guess, he was a collie-dog. He lived in a yard, and he had a big kennel to himself, because he was a big dog. He was on a chain, because he had to guard his master's house, and Mr. Snoot didn't want him wandering about loose, far away from the house.

So Collie was always tied up except when Mr. Snoot took him out for a walk. He was often very bored. It wasn't much fun to sit night and day inside or outside his kennel, when he wanted to go and hunt rabbits or see his friends. All he could do was to bark loudly when any stranger came to the yard.

That was what Mr. Snoot wanted him to do. Mr. Snoot was a miser, and he had a good deal of money hidden up the chimney-place in his kitchen. As soon as he heard Collie bark he was warned of people coming, and he could look out for them.

When the winter came Mr. Snoot put more blankets on his bed. He bought extra milk from the milkman, so that he could warm it up at night and put it beside his bed in a flask to keep it hot. He had a tin of his favourite biscuits there too, to eat with the hot milk. He didn't mind waking up at night then, for he would pour himself out a glass of hot milk and eat a few biscuits. Then he would pop down into his kitchen, put his hand up the chimney, feel to see if his money-bag was there, and go back to bed again, quite happy.

He would pull his lovely warm blankets over his head, and go peacefully to sleep, knowing that if any tramp or robber came along, Collie would bark loudly to tell him.

The days were cold. The nights were colder. Collie had some straw in his kennel to lie on, but not much, and what there was was rather flattened down by the weight of his big body. He shivered. It made his chain rattle when he shivered. He got further into his kennel and tried to spread the straw round himself, but there wasn't enough.

He went out to his bowl to get a drink, and to see if there were any biscuits left. Perhaps a meal would warm him up a bit. But alas, the water had frozen hard. His dinner-bowl was quite empty.

Poor Collie! He went back into his kennel, and wished that Mr. Snoot had swung it round to face the other way, because the cold north wind came blowing straight into the kennel. How could a dog possibly get warm with a wind like that blowing at him all the time!

Collie felt colder and colder. He shivered more and more. Then he felt a sneeze coming. It was a big one. "A-a-a-a-a-WHOOOOOOSH-ooooo!" sneezed Collie loudly.

There was a squeal from outside, a squeal of fright. Then a little voice said, "What did you do that for? You blew me off my feet!"

Collie stuck his nose outside in surprise. Who was this? He hadn't heard anyone. Ought he to bark?

Outside stood a small man, dressed in a brown tunic, and brown stockings and shoes. He wore a pointed hat, and had a long grey beard. His bright blue eyes twinkled like stars on a frosty night.

"Hallo!" said Collie surprised. "One of the little folk, I suppose? What are you doing here at this time of night?"

"I got called out to a robin who's half-frozen," said the brownie. "I'm a doctor, you know. Dr. Help-a-Bit. You may have heard of me."

"Well, I haven't really," said Collie. "Did I almost blow you off your feet just now when I sneezed?"

"Right off," said Dr. Help-a-Bit. "I got an awful shock. What's the matter with you, sneezing like that? And why do you keep rattling your chain?"

"Well, brownie, I don't mean to rattle my chain, but I can't help it, because I'm so cold," said Collie. "It's my shivering that rattles the chain."

"What a shame!" said the brownie. "Get out of your kennel, and go and bark at the house door. They'll have to let you in then."

"I can't," said Collie. "I'm chained. Can't you see? I'm terribly cold because I can't run about to keep myself warm, and I haven't enough straw to cuddle down in."

"I can't have this sort of thing," said Dr. Help-a-Bit, looking very fierce all of a sudden. "I'll go and see your master about it. Poor creature! How can anyone treat you like that? I'll go and wake your master."

Before Collie could stop him the brownie had gone to the back door, opened it with a key he had and gone inside. He went upstairs, drawn there by a loud noise of snoring. He came to Mr. Snoot's bedroom. By the light of the little lamp that Mr. Snoot always left burning, the brownie saw the fat old man lying fast asleep in bed.

"Wake up," said the brownie sternly. Mr. Snoot didn't stir. The brownie gave him a prod. Still Mr. Snoot didn't wake. Then Dr. Help-a-Bit's eyes gleamed.

He had noticed the great pile of warm, woolly blankets that Mr. Snoot had on his bed. He saw the flask of hot milk by the bedside and the tin of biscuits. How pleased a cold and hungry dog would be with all those things.

The brownie put the tin of biscuits in one pocket and the flask of

hot milk into another. Then, softly pulling at the pile of woolly blankets, he dragged them all off the bed, tucked them round his shoulders to carry, and went downstairs again. Mr. Snoot had nothing on him except for a thin sheet. All his blankets had gone.

Dr. Help-a-Bit took everything outside. "Here you are," he said to Collie, pouring the milk into the bowl. "Drink it up while it's hot. And eat these biscuits too—you'll like them. Then I'll pack your kennel with these fine blankets and you'll be as warm as toast, as soon as you cuddle down in them."

Collie was overjoyed. He lapped up the hot milk. He crunched up the delicious biscuits. Then he squeezed into the fleecy blankets and the brownie pulled them closely round him. "I'm sorry I'm not strong enough to swing your kennel away from the cold north wind," he said. "But I don't somehow think you'll feel the cold now!"

Collie didn't! He slept all night long in warmth and comfort, a very happy dog. How kind of the brownie to bother about him like that! Collie wished he could do something in return, but he couldn't think of anything.

Now about half an hour later, Mr. Snoot awoke shivering with cold. He put out his hand and felt for his blankets. They weren't there.

They must have fallen on the floor, he thought. He sat up and looked. What a very extraordinary thing—they weren't on the floor either. In fact, they were nowhere to be seen.

Cold, puzzled and frightened, Mr. Snoot took up his flask to pour out a glass of hot milk. It was empty! The brownie had carefully taken it back with the biscuit tin and put them in their place beside Mr. Snoot's bed. No biscuits—no milk—no blankets! Mr. Snoot was alarmed. He thought there must surely be burglars about—and yet Collie hadn't barked!

He crept downstairs and felt for his money-bag up the chimney. It was still there. He pulled it down, and dragged it upstairs. He locked the door and looked round for a bed-covering. There was nothing he could use except for a table-cloth, and that wasn't very warm! So Mr. Snoot shivered all night long, and couldn't sleep at all.

In the morning he went to scold Collie for letting a thief come in the night without barking at him. He saw something in Collie's kennel, and *how* astonished he was to find that all his blankets were stuffed there! He pulled them out in amazement.

"Who did this?" he said sternly to Collie. "It couldn't have been you because you are always chained up. It's a very silly joke, whoever did it. I am not pleased."

Well, as he had taken the blankets away, poor Collie was as cold as ever the next night. But along came the brownie again to see if he was all right—and how angry he was when he found that Mr. Snoot had taken away the blankets, but hadn't bothered to give poor Collie any more straw—or even water instead of the ice in his bowl.

"Well, Snoot can shiver all night again," he said, grimly. "I'm going to get his blankets, his hot milk and his biscuits once more!"

So into the house he went, up the stairs and into the bedroom. Once again he pulled the blankets off the snoring Mr. Snoot, and took his flask of hot milk and his biscuits. And once again Collie lapped eagerly, crunched the biscuits and then snuggled down in the blankets.

And once more poor Mr. Snoot awoke shivering with the cold, and looked for the blankets that were not there! He was really very frightened when he found that they had disappeared once again!

He lighted a lantern, put on his dressing-gown, and went downstairs and out into the yard. Yes, just as he had thought, Collie had his blankets again; and what was this in his bowl—a drop of milk—and a few crumbs of his best biscuits! So that was where his things were going! Mr. Snoot was angry.

He tried to pull the blankets out of Collie's kennel. But Collie held on to them, and it looked as if they would be torn to pieces!

"I *must* have my blankets!" roared Mr. Snoot. "I shall freeze at night if I don't."

"And what about your dog, you selfish fellow?" said a stern voice nearby. Mr. Snoot turned and saw the brownie looking at him. "Hardly any straw in his bitterly cold kennel, no water to drink—shivering all night long, poor thing. You ought to be ashamed of yourself. Collie, let go the blanket. I've got an idea!"

Collie let go. Mr. Snoot bent to snatch them, but the brownie took them first. He glared at Mr. Snoot. "You'll stay out here in this yard all night long, and see what it is like! I'm going to take Collie upstairs and put him into your bed and cover him with these blankets. You stay here and pretend to be him. See how you like it!"

Mr. Snoot watched the brownie and Collie going indoors. Dr. Help-a-Bit had undone the chain, so Collie was free. Mr. Snoot tried to go after them, but the brownie had put magic into his slippers and he couldn't move a step out of the cold, windy yard.

Weeping with the cold, Mr. Snoot crept into the kennel to try and get a bit warmer. But the north wind blew in strongly. There was too little straw to nestle in. He shivered so much that the kennel creaked all night long.

But Collie slept well, tucked in Mr. Snoot's comfortable bed. What a night he had! Mr. Snoot found him there in the morning when he went upstairs. The magic went from his slippers at dawn, and he was able to go into the house.

Collie awoke and looked at him, expecting him to be very angry.

But Mr. Snoot wasn't. He was strangely humble. He spoke to Collie. "I didn't know how cold it was out there without enough straw. I didn't know how the wind blew into your kennel. I didn't see that your water was frozen. I beg your pardon. Forgive me. I have had a most dreadful night, the kind of night you must often have had. Poor Collie!"

Collie licked Mr. Snoot's hand. And that day Mr. Snoot filled the kennel with warm straw and swung it right away from the wind. He put fresh water down and a big dish of biscuits and bones. He didn't put Collie on the chain again.

Collie spoke to the brownie gratefully when he next saw him. "Thank you!" he said. "I'm very happy now—and all because I did that very big sneeze one night and blew you off your feet!"

Wanted—A Chatter-Box

ONCE THE little Prince of Heyho fell very ill, and lay in bed for many weeks. When he grew better he was allowed to sit up for a few minutes each day—but, oh, how bored he was because he was not allowed to do anything at all!

"I mustn't read! I mustn't play with my soldiers! I mustn't do my jigsaws! It's always: I mustn't! I mustn't! I mustn't!" he said crossly. "I'm so bored. I'm so dull."

"You could have your musical-box," said his nurse. "You like that, don't you?"

"Yes," said the little prince, and his nurse fetched it for him. She set it going by winding the key at the bottom of the box. She put it on the bed, and it began to tinkle out its pretty tunes.

"Now, you are not to wind it up when it runs down," said his nurse. "I will do that for you."

The little prince lay and listened to the music. He liked it. But very soon the musical-box needed winding again. He called for his nurse, but she wasn't there. Bother! Now he would have to lie with nothing to do, nothing to listen to again! He kicked out crossly—and the box fell off the bed with a crash. Oh dear! Was it broken?

When his nurse came back again she picked up the box. "Did it fall off?" she said. "Oh, I do hope it hasn't broken!"

But it was. It was very sad, and the prince cried about it. It was the nicest musical-box in the kingdom.

"Never mind," said his nurse. "I'll see if I can get you another."

So she did—but the tunes were silly and the little prince quickly got bored with them. He kicked the box off the bed—and that was broken, too.

"You're naughty," said his nurse. "I shan't get you another one."

That afternoon, when the prince was supposed to be fast asleep, he heard tapping at his window. Then a small, long-eared head peeped in. It was Big-Eyes, the pixie who used to play with the prince when he was well.

"Can't stop a minute!" he said in a whisper. "Just came to see how you are, little prince."

"Bored and dull," said the prince, and tears ran down his cheeks. "I've had two musical-boxes and they're both broken. Anyway, they only play music. I'd like a box that could say things to me—go on and on like a musical-box, but could *tell* me things instead of playing music."

"Well—I've heard of Chatter-Boxes," said Big-Eyes. "Have you? Shall I see if I can get you a Chatter-Box? It should be full of chatter and talk—you wouldn't be bored if you had a Chatter-Box, would you?"

"Oh, that does sound a good idea," said the little prince, cheering up. "Get me a Chatter-Box, Big-Eyes, do. A nice big one, full of chatter and talk."

Big-Eyes slid down from the window, almost tumbling out of the big pear tree he was in. He jumped to the ground and stood there, thinking hard, his ears sticking straight up. Where could he get a Chatter-Box? A box that would talk and talk and talk!

"I've never heard of one in Heyho Land," he thought. "But there may be one in the land of boys and girls. They have all sorts of wonderful things there. I might be able to buy a Chatter-Box there."

So off he went to our land, and began to poke about in the shops. He wore a big hat to cover up his pixie ears, and most people thought he was a rather queer-looking little boy.

"What do you want?" asked the shopman at a big toy shop. "Those are all musical-boxes there. Do stop winding them up. I'm tired of the noise. Do you want to buy one?"

"Well—I don't want a *musical*-box," said Big-Eyes. "I'm really looking for a Chatter-Box."

The man laughed. "A chatterbox! What a queer little fellow you are, to be sure! Chatterboxes aren't sold in shops, you know."

"Where can I get one, then?" asked Big-Eyes.

The man laughed again. "Well, my boy," he said, "if you want to hear one you go to that house up the hill there—the one with the red curtains. You'll find a little girl there called Polly. She's a chatterbox all right. Never stops talking day or night!"

"Thank you," said Big-Eyes, surprised to hear that a *little girl* could be a Chatter-Box. "I'll go and listen to her. She may be just what I want."

So off he went to the house with red curtains. He squeezed in at an open window and stood listening in a little room.

From somewhere not far away there came a pretty little voice.

"And, Mummy, it was such a nice little cat I couldn't help stroking it, and it said 'Miaow, miaow,' just like that and I'm sure it liked me, so I went to the milkman and I asked him for a saucer of milk, and do you know he gave me one, but when I got back to where I'd left the cat it was gone so I had to give the milk to a dog I met and he was very naughty, he broke the saucer the milkman gave me and——"

"Polly, do stop chattering for a moment!" said another voice. "I'm trying to read."

"Oh, Mummy, what are you reading? I do hope it's something exciting, then you can tell me about it," said Polly's voice. "I won't talk for a minute, then—but oh, I must tell you about something I read yesterday. Do you know, I read in my book that——"

"Be quiet, Polly, darling," said her mother. "I never in my life knew such a little chatterbox."

"Oh dear—I've got such a lot to say and nobody ever wants to hear it!" sighed Polly. "Well, I'll talk to my dolls instead. Angela, come here. Sit up nicely. That's right. Now, did I ever tell you about a doll I once had whose eyes got shut and wouldn't open, and——"

"POLLY! *Will* you stop talking for a minute?" cried her mother. "Chatter, chatter, chatter, all day long—and you even talk in your sleep. Be quiet, you little chatterbox."

Big-Eyes had been listening with great interest. He longed to know what had happened to the doll with shut eyes. He thought that he could listen to Polly all day long. What a *lovely* Chatter-Box! He hid himself behind a curtain and waited for Polly's mother to leave Polly by herself.

As soon as the mother had gone into the kitchen Big-Eyes slipped into the nursery, wondering what kind of a girl this Chatter-Box was. Perhaps she lived in a big box?

No, she didn't. There she was, quite an ordinary little girl, nursing a doll. She looked up in surprise at Big-Eyes.

"Little girl, I want you to come with me," said Big-Eyes. "I'm looking for a Chatter-Box to take to the little Prince of Heyho. He's ill and bored—he'll love to listen to you."

"But I don't want to come with you!" said Polly in alarm. "I'll call my mother if you make me go!"

Big-Eyes didn't let her call her mother. He muttered a few magic words and Polly's eyes closed at once. She put her head down on the table and slept. Big-Eyes touched her with his little magic wand and she grew small—as small as Angela, her doll! How queer she looked, poor little Polly.

Big-Eyes looked round for something to put her in to carry her away. He saw a cardboard box in a corner. Just the thing! He lifted the tiny Polly and put her carefully into the box. He made some little holes in it for her to breathe fresh air. Then he ran out of the room with the box in his arms. It wasn't long before he got back to the palace and climbed up the pear-tree to the window. He put the box on the bed and grinned at the little prince.

"I've brought you a Chatter-Box. The chatter is inside. It's asleep at present, but when it wakes up it will talk all day long. This is a real proper Chatter-Box!"

Well, when Polly woke up she had quite a lot to say. She tried to get out of the box. She couldn't, of course, and she began to talk fast.

"Let me out, it's not fair to keep me in here, I feel like a caterpillar or something, shut up in a box, and I don't like it. I know what a caterpillar feels like now, and it reminds me of some I once had. They were silkworms and I didn't shut them up in a box, I left off the lid, but some sparrows came or some thrushes, I don't know which, and they saw my lovely silkworms and they gobbled them all up and when I came back——"

The little prince listened in delight. "It's a lovely Chatter-Box," he said. "I do like it. Go on, Chatter-Box."

"Who are you, I'd like to know, talking to me like that?" said Polly, crossly. "You let me out of this box. It smells of soap or something. I shall smell of soap, too, and I would rather smell of lavender water, I've got some in a little bottle that Granny gave me for my birthday and she gave me a teddy bear too, but he hasn't a growl any more, it suddenly went, I think somebody must have trodden on him, poor thing . . ."

"Oh, go on, go on," begged the little prince, feeling most interested.

"What do you mean, go on, go on?" said Polly, from inside the box, still feeling puzzled and annoyed. "Go on, go on, indeed, as if I was a railway train or a motor-car rushing down the road! I wish I was, then I'd rush back home and go in at the back door, but perhaps I couldn't if I was a train, I should frighten Mummy too much and I might even knock down the walls, and certainly the cat would be scared out of her life and she might desert her kittens, she's got three, and they're so sweet, especially the ginger one who hasn't got a name."

"Call him Marmalade," said the little prince, more and more interested.

There was a snort from inside the box. "What a name for a kitten! Might as well call him Apricot Jam. Who are you, talking away to me like that? You let me out or I'll break this box to pieces, and——"

"It's a perfectly LOVELY Chatter-Box," said the little prince. "It goes on and on and on—I don't expect it will ever stop, Big-Eyes. I shall never be dull or bored now, never!"

Nurse was very surprised when she came in and heard the voice from the box.

"It's my new Chatter-Box," explained the prince. "It goes on and on like that, telling me all kinds of things. I love it. Don't take it away, Nurse. Big-Eyes brought it for me."

Well, all that day, and half the night too, Polly chattered away. She felt very hungry, but it didn't occur to anyone that Chatter-Boxes needed food, any more than musical-boxes did. The little prince thought it was marvellous that his new toy didn't even need winding up.

In the morning Polly awoke, stiff and uncomfortable and very, very hungry. She battered at the box and began to shout loudly.

"Let me out, let me out! Why have you put me in here like this? Why do you keep me a prisoner? I want to go home, I want my breakfast, I want my mother, let me out!"

"Are you alive, then? Aren't you a *toy* Chatter-Box?" cried the little prince. "Are you really somebody?"

"Of course I'm somebody. I'm Polly Jones, and I want to go home!" shouted Polly. "Let me out! Why have you put me here?"

When Big-Eyes arrived he found the little prince looking worried. "My Chatter-Box isn't a toy," he said. "It's somebody real. We'd better open the box."

"Of course it's somebody real," said Big-Eyes. "It's a little girl called Polly. She's a marvellous Chatter-Box; that's why I caught her, made her small and shut her up in this box to chatter to you. She can't stop. Her tongue is never still. We will keep her here till you are better. I'll put a little bread and milk for her into the box today."

Polly had heard all this. Her heart almost stopped in fright. What! She had been made small—and put into this box—and made a prisoner so that she could amuse somebody? Then she wouldn't say another word!

So she shut her lips tightly and was quite silent. "Talk!" cried the

little prince, tapping the box. "Chatter away! Tell me things!"

No sound from the box at all. Big-Eyes tapped too. "Chatter, chatter, chatter!" he commanded. No sound came out. Not a word! Big-Eyes opened the box and looked inside.

"Perhaps she's run down," said the prince. "Can she be wound up?"

"No. She hasn't a key," said Big-Eyes. "I do hope she chatters soon."

But Polly didn't. She was afraid to, in case they kept her there. She hoped Big-Eyes would take her home if she didn't say a single word.

And that is just what he did. He carried her back in the box, and opened it, and made her grow to her own size again. She was so glad!

"Oh, thank you!" she cried. "It was dreadful to be put into a box and taken away, just because I was such a chatterbox. I've never been quiet for so long before. You were bad to do all that to me. I shan't chatter so much again."

"Oh—you're talking again now," said Big-Eyes in delight. "I've a good mind to make you small again."

"It wouldn't be any good," said Polly. "I should just close my mouth and not say a word. But if you like to show me the way I'll come with you to-morrow and talk to the little prince, so that he won't be quite so dull. But please, please don't ever put me into a box again!"

So she went to visit the prince and talked to him and played games, so that he wasn't dull any more and soon felt much better.

And Polly didn't talk *quite* so much at home after that! Her mother had only to say, "Oh, Polly, don't be such a *chatterbox*!" and Polly would shut her lips and not say another word. She didn't want to be a box of chatter again—no, she'd soon show her mother that she *could* be quiet if she wanted to.

Are *you* a chatterbox? You are? Well, do look out for Big-Eyes, then. He'll love to know you and take you to the little prince! I expect you'd love it too!

The Humpy Goblin's Kettle

MISTER CURLY was a small pixie who lived all by himself in Twisty Cottage. His cottage stood at the end of the Village of Ho, and was always very neatly kept. It had blue and yellow curtains at the windows and blue and yellow flowers in the garden.

Mister Curly was mean. He was the meanest pixie that ever lived, but he always pretended to be very generous indeed. If he had a bag of peppermints he never let anyone see it, but put it straight into his pocket till he got home. And if he met any of the other pixies he would pull a long face and say:

"If only I had a bag of sweets I would offer you one."

"Never mind," the others said. "It's nice of you to *think* of it!"

And they went off saying what a nice, generous creature Mister Curly was!

Now one day, as Mister Curly was walking home along Dimity Lane, where the trees met overhead, so that it was just like walking in a green tunnel, he saw a queer fellow in front of him. This was a Humpy Goblin, and he carried a great many saucepans, kettles and pans, all slung down his back, round his shoulders and over his chest.

They made a great noise as he walked, but louder than the noise was the Humpy Goblin's voice. He sang all the time in a voice like a cracked bell:

"Do you want a saucepan, kettle or pan?
If you do, here's the Goblin Man,
The Humpy Goblin with his load
Of pots and pans is down the road,
Hie, hie hie, here's the Goblin Man,
Do you want a saucepan, kettle or pan?"

Now Mister Curly badly wanted a new kettle, because his own had a hole in it and the water leaked over his stove each day, making a funny hissing noise. So he ran after the Goblin Man, and called him. The Humpy Goblin turned round and grinned. He was a cheerful fellow, always pleased to see anybody.

"I want a good little kettle, nice and cheap," said Curly.

"I've just the one for you," said Humpy, and he pointed to a bright little kettle on his back. Curly looked at it.

"How much is it?" he asked.

"Six pence," said the Goblin. This was quite cheap, but mean old Curly wasn't going to give six pence for the kettle. He pretended to be shocked at the price, and then he gave a huge sigh.

"Oh, I'm not rich enough to pay all that," he said, sadly. "I can only pay three pence."

"Oh, no," said Humpy, firmly. "Three pence isn't enough."

Well, they stood and talked to one another for a long time, one saying six pence and the other saying three pence, until at last the Humpy Goblin laughed in Curly's face and walked off, jingling all his kettles and pans.

"You're a mean old stick!" he called after Curly. "I'm not going to sell you anything! Good-bye, Mister Mean!"

Off he went and soon began to sing his song again. Curly heard him.

"Do you want a saucepan, kettle or pan?
If you do, here's the Goblin Man!"

Curly stood and watched him angrily. Then he started walking too. He had to follow the Goblin Man because that was the way home to Twisty Cottage. But he took care not to follow too close, for he was afraid that Humpy might call something rude after him.

It was a hot day and the Goblin was tired. After a while he thought he would sit down in the hedge and rest. So down he sat—and it wasn't more than a minute before he was sound asleep and snoring! Curly heard him and knew he must be sound asleep. A naughty thought slipped into his head.

"I wonder if I could take that kettle from him whilst he's asleep? I could leave three pence beside him to pay for it. How cross he would be when he woke up to find that I had got the kettle for three pence after all!"

He crept up to the Humpy Goblin. He certainly was sound asleep, and his mouth was so wide open that it was a good thing there wasn't anything above his head that could drop into it. Curly carefully undid the little shining kettle without making even a clink of noise. Then he put three bright pennies on the grass beside the Goblin, and ran off, chuckling to himself for being so smart.

He soon reached home. He filled the little kettle with water and put it on the fire. It really was a dear little thing, and it boiled very quickly indeed, sending a spurt of steam out of the spout almost before Curly had got out the teapot to make the tea.

Just as he was sitting down to enjoy a cup of tea and a piece of cake someone walked up his garden path and looked in at the door. It was the Humpy Goblin. When he saw that Curly had the kettle on the fire, he grinned all over his face.

"So you've got it!" he said. "Well, much good may it do you! Kettle, listen to me! Teach Mister Curly the lesson he needs! Ho, ho, Curly, keep the kettle! I don't want it!"

Laughing and skipping the Goblin went down the path again. Curly felt a bit uncomfortable. What was he laughing like that for?

"Oh, he just tried to frighten me and make me think something nasty would happen," said Curly to himself. "Silly old Goblin!"

He cleared away his cup and saucer and filled up the kettle again. He was washing up the dirty dishes when a knock came at his door, and Dame Pitapat looked in.

"I say, Curly, could you let me have a little tea? I've emptied my tin and it's such a long way to the shops."

Now Curly had a whole tin full, but he wasn't going to let Dame Pitapat have any. He ran to the dresser and took down a tin he knew was empty.

"Yes, certainly, Dame Pitapat," he said, "you shall have some of my tea. Oh dear! The tin's empty! What a pity! You could have had half of it if only I'd had any, but I must have used it all up!"

Dame Pitapat looked at the empty tin. Then she turned to go.

"I'm sorry I bothered you, Curly," she said. "It was kind of you to say I could have had half, if only you'd had any tea!"

Then a funny thing happened. The little kettle on the stove sent out a big spurt of steam and began to shout a shrill song:

50

"Mister Curly has plenty of tea!
    He's just as mean as a pixie can be!
    Look in the tin on the left of the shelf
    And see what a lot he has for himself!"

Then the kettle took another breath and shouted: "Mean old thing! Stingy old thing! Oooooh, look at him!"

Dame Pitapat was so astonished that she stood gaping for quite a minute. She couldn't think where the song came from. She had no idea it was the kettle on the stove. But Curly knew it was, and he was so angry and ashamed that he could have cried.

Dame Pitapat went to the shelf and took down the tin that stood on the left. She opened it and sure enough it was full to the brim.

"Oh, look at this!" she said. "Well, Curly, you said I could have half of any tea you had, so I shall take you at your word. Thanks very much."

She emptied half the tea out into the tin she had brought and went out of the cottage, looking round curiously to see if she could spy who had sung that song about Curly.

Curly was so angry with the kettle that he decided to beat it with a stick. But before he could do that someone poked his head in at the window and called him.

"Mister Curly! Will you lend me your umbrella, please? I've lost mine and it's raining."

It was little Capers, the pixie who lived next door. He was always lending Curly things, and now he had come to borrow something himself. But Curly was in a very bad temper.

"My umbrella's lost too," he said. "I'm so sorry, Capers. You could have it if only I had it myself, but it's gone."

"Oh, well, never mind," said Capers. "It's nice of you to say you would have lent it to me."

Before he could go, the shining kettle gave a tiny hop on the stove and began to sing again:

"Mister Curly has got an umbrella,
　He's such a mean and stingy fella,
　He says he hasn't got one at all,
　But just you go and look in the hall!"

Then it took another breath and began to shout again at the top of its steamy voice: "Mean old thing! Stingy old thing! Oooooh, look at him!"

Capers was so surprised to hear this song that he nearly fell in at the window. He stared at Curly, who was looking as black as thunder and as red as a beetroot. Then Capers looked through the kitchen door into the tiny hall—and sure enough Curly's green umbrella stood there.

Capers jumped in at the window and fetched the umbrella. He waved it at Curly.

"You said I could have it if only you had got it!" he cried. "Here it is, so I'll borrow it! Many thanks!"

He ran off and left Curly nearly crying with rage. The pixie caught up a stick and ran to beat the kettle—but that small kettle was far too quick for him! It rose up in the air and put itself high up on a shelf for safety. Then it poured just a drop of boiling water on to Curly's hand, which made the pixie dance and shout with pain.

"You wait till I get you!" cried Curly, shaking his stick.

Someone knocked at his front door. Curly opened it.

Rag and Tag the two gnomes stood there, smiling.

"Mister Curly, we are collecting pennies for poor Mister Tumble whose house was burnt down yesterday," they said. "You are so generous that we thought you would be sure to give us one."

Curly knew that there was no money in his pockets, so he pulled them inside out quickly, saying: "Oh, yes, you shall have whatever money I have, Rag and Tag. Goodness, there's none in this pocket— and none in that! How unfortunate! I haven't any pennies to give you, and I should have been *so* pleased to have let you have all I had!"

"Well, that's very nice of you to say so," said Rag and Tag. "Never mind. Thank you very much for *trying* to be generous!"

Before they could go, that little kettle was singing again, spurting out great clouds of steam as it did so:

"Although he says he hasn't any,
    Curly's got a silver penny!
    Look in his purse on the table there,
    And take the money he well can spare!"

Then, taking another breath, the kettle shouted with all its might:

54

"Mean old thing! Stingy old thing! Oooooh, look at him!"

Rag and Tag stared all round the kitchen to see where the voice came from, but they couldn't see anyone but Curly. It couldn't be the pixie singing, surely! No, he looked too angry and ashamed to sing anything!

The gnomes saw the purse lying on the table and they ran for it. Inside was a silver coin. They took it and put it into their box.

"Well, Curly," they said, "you said we might have any pennies you had if you'd had any—and you have, so we'll take this silver one. Good-bye!"

Out they went, giggling together, wondering who it was in the cottage that had given Curly away.

As for Curly, he was so angry that he caught up a jug and flung it straight at the kettle, which was still high up on the shelf. Crash! The kettle hopped aside and the jug broke in a dozen pieces against the wall behind. The milk spilt and dripped on to Curly's head. Then the kettle began to laugh, and you can't think how angry that made Curly!

He took up a hammer and flung that at the kettle too—but once more it slipped to one side, and oh dear me, smash went a lovely big

jar of plum jam up on the shelf. It all splashed down on to Curly, so what with milk and jam he was a fine sight. The kettle nearly killed itself with laughing. It almost fell off the shelf.

Curly went and washed himself under the tap. He felt frightened. What was he going to do with that awful singing kettle? He must get rid of it somehow, or it would tell everyone the most dreadful tales about him.

"I'll wait till tonight," thought Curly. "Then, when it's asleep I'll take it and throw it away."

So he took no more notice of the kettle, and as no other visitors came that day the kettle was fairly quiet, except that sometimes it would suddenly shout: "Mean old thing! Stingy old thing! Ooooooh, look at him!" Then Curly would almost jump out of his skin with fright, and glare at the kettle angrily.

At nine o'clock Curly went to bed. The kettle hopped down to the stove and went to sleep. Curly waited for a little while, and then he crept out of bed. He went to the stove and took hold of the kettle. Ah, he had it now! The kettle woke up and shouted, but Curly had it by the handle. The water in it was no longer hot, so it could not hurt.

The pixie hurried outside with the kettle and went to the bottom of his garden. There was a rubbish-heap there and the pixie stuffed the struggling kettle right into the middle. He left it there and went back delighted. He climbed into bed and fell asleep.

But at midnight something woke him by tapping at the window.

"Let me in!" cried a voice. "Let me in! I'm all dirty and I want washing!"

"That's that horrid kettle!" thought Curly, in a fright. "Well, it can go on tapping! I won't let it in!"

But the kettle tapped and tapped and at last it flung itself hard against the glass, broke it and came in through the hole! It went over to Curly's bed and stood itself there.

"Wash me!" it said. "I'm dirty and smelly. You shouldn't have put me on that nasty rubbish-heap!"

"Get off my nice clean bed!" cried Curly, angrily. "Look what a mess you are making!"

But the kettle wouldn't get off, and in the end the angry pixie had to get up and wash the kettle till it was clean again. Then he banged it down on the stove and left it.

Next day the kettle sang songs about him again, and Curly kept

hearing it shout: "Mean old fellow! Stingy old fellow! Ooooooh, look at him!" till he was tired of it. So many people had heard about the strange things happening in the pixie's cottage that all day long visitors came to ask for different things, and poor Curly was nearly worried out of his life.

"I'll drown that kettle in my well tonight!" he thought. So once more he took the kettle when it was asleep, and threw it down the well. Splash! Ha, it wouldn't get out of there in a hurry!

But about three o'clock in the morning there came a tap-tap-tap at the window, which had been mended. It was the kettle back again!

"Curly! Let me in! I'm c-c-c-c-cold and w-wet! Let me in!"

Curly was afraid his window would be broken again, so he jumped out of bed and let in the shivering kettle. To his horror it crept into bed with him and wouldn't go away!

"It was cold and wet in the well!" said the kettle.

So Curly had to warm the kettle and how angry he was! It was so uncomfortable to sleep with a kettle, especially one that kept sticking its sharp spout into him. But he had to put up with it. In the morning he put the kettle back on the stove and started to think hard whilst he had his breakfast.

"I can't get rid of that kettle," he said to himself. "And while it's here it's sure to sing horrid things about me every time anyone comes to borrow something. I wonder what it would do if I let people have what they ask for? I'll try and see."

So when Mother Homey came and begged for a bit of soap, because she had run out of it and the shops were closed that afternoon, Curly gave her a whole new piece without making any excuse at all. Mother Homey was surprised and delighted.

"Thank you so much," she said. "You're a kind soul, Curly."

The kettle said nothing at all. Not a single word.

As for Curly, he suddenly felt very nice inside. It was lovely to give somebody something. It made him feel warm and kind. He made up his mind to do it again to see if he felt nice the next time—and to see if that wretched kettle said anything.

He soon found that the kettle said never a word unless he was mean or untruthful—and he found too that it was lovely to be kind and to give things away; it was nice even to lend them.

"I've been horrid and nasty," thought Curly to himself. "I'll turn over a new leaf and try to be different. And that old kettle can say what it likes! Anyway, it boils very quickly and makes a lovely pot of tea."

Very soon the kettle found little to say, for Curly became kind and generous. Once or twice he forgot, but as soon as he heard the kettle beginning to speak he quickly remembered, and the kettle stopped its song.

And one day who should peep in at the door but the Humpy Goblin, grinning all over his face as usual.

"Hallo, Curly!" he said. "How did you like the kettle? Was it cheap for three pence? I've come to take the kettle back, if you want to get rid of it. It was a mean trick to play on you, really, but I think you deserved it!"

Curly looked at the smiling goblin. Then he took his purse from his pocket and found three pennies. He held them out to the Humpy Goblin.

"Here you are," he said. "You wanted six pence for the kettle and I was mean enough to leave you only three pence. Here's the other three pence."

"But—but—don't you want to give me back the kettle?" asked Humpy, in surprise. "I left a horrid singing spell in it."

"Yes, I know," said Curly. "But I deserved it. I'm different now. I like the kettle, too—we're friends. I try to be kind now, so the kettle doesn't sing nasty things about me. It just hums nice, friendly little songs. And it makes a wonderful pot of tea."

"Well, well, well, wonders will never end!" said the Goblin Man, astonished. "Don't bother about the other three pence, Curly. I don't want it."

"Well, if you won't take it, let me offer you a cup of tea made from water boiled in the singing kettle," said Curly. Humpy was even more astonished to hear the pixie being so kind, but he sat down at the table in delight.

Then he and Curly had a cup of tea each and a large slice of ginger cake—and they talked together and found that they liked one another very much indeed.

So now Mister Curly and the Humpy Goblin are the very greatest friends, and the little singing kettle hums its loudest when it boils water for their tea. You should just hear it.